Passion and Poison

TALES OF SHAPE-SHIFTERS, GHOSTS, AND SPIRITED WOMEN

by Janice M. Del Negro

drawings by Vince Natale

Marshall Cavendish

Text copyright © 2007 by Janice M. Del Negro
Illustrations copyright © 2007 by Marshall Cavendish

Marshall Cavendish Corporation
99 White Plains Road
Tarrytown, NY 10591
www.marshallcavendish.us/kids

This book is a work of fiction. Names, characters, places, and incidents are products of the
author's imagination and are used fictitiously. Any resemblance to actual events or locales or
persons, living or dead, is entirely coincidental.

Library of Congress Cataloging-in-Publication Data
Del Negro, Janice.
Passion and poison ; tales of shape-shifters, ghosts, and spirited women / by Janice M. Del
Negro. — 1st ed.
p. cm.
Contents: The bargain — Rosie Hopewell — Skulls and bones, ghosts and gold -- The severed
hand — Rubies — Seachild — Hide and seek.
ISBN 978-0-7614-5361-1
1. Tales. 2. Short stories, American. 3. Ghost stories, American. 4. Supernatural—Fiction. [1.
Folklore. 2. Ghosts—Fiction. 3. Supernatural—Fiction. 4. Short stories.] I. Title.
PZ8.1.D372Pas 2007
[398.2]—dc22
2007007237

The text of this book is set in Caxton.
Book design by Anahid Hamparian
Editor: Margery Cuyler

Printed in China
First edition
10 9 8 7 6 5 4 3 2

mc Marshall Cavendish

To Miranda, who loves things that go
bump in the night, and to Bonnie, who doesn't

Contents

ONE
The Bargain

Elizabeth Frye blew into town like a chill wind. At least, that's what the women whispered behind her back. There was just something about her. Oh, the men didn't think so. No, the men, they liked Elizabeth. She had skin like ripe peaches and hair like sun on yellow roses. As a matter of fact, the men liked Elizabeth just fine.

But the women didn't like her. Not one of them could quite put her finger on why. There was just something about Elizabeth that made them want to pull their skirts aside when she passed, to hide their children.

It was only natural that the men would go out of their way to help a young widow adjust to life in their small town, and it was only natural that Elizabeth Frye would accept their help, with a smile of gratitude in her bright eyes. The men never could say enough about Elizabeth's bright eyes. They could never agree on what color they were, either. Like water, her eyes changed with every trick of the light. The women could have told them, if they'd had sense enough to ask. The women knew the color of her eyes, all right—gray, the color of ice frozen over dark water. The men laughed when the women called Elizabeth "that stranger," and said when some fine fellow made her a respectable married matron instead of an attractive young widow, the women would come around.

But they never did. Not even when Elizabeth's eye

finally brightened on a young man, because the man Elizabeth finally favored didn't seem her kind at all.

Johnny Drummond was a hard-working man who kept to himself. His mother had died some years before, leaving him one younger brother and a run-down farm. She'd made Johnny promise to raise the boy right, and he'd no trouble with that. The brothers were close—they were all each other had, really. The only thing of earthly value Johnny's mother left him was a silver cup she had cherished all her life. Both her sons had been christened with it. John was not a sentimental man. Still, every Sunday he would take his mother's christening cup to the well by the back fence, and standing there as the sun came up, he'd drink some water and say a prayer. It was a way of keeping faith with his promise. It wasn't something he ever told anyone. After all, he was a hard-working man who kept to himself.

John wasn't a religious man. At least, he didn't go to church on Sundays. He worked. When he'd inherited the property, several men made him offers, but John wouldn't sell. Even in his earliest grief, he wouldn't sell. He worked. He worked hard. When John's younger brother was old enough, he worked, too. By the time Elizabeth Frye came to town, Johnny Drummond was on his way to being surprisingly well-off, more well-off than anyone had ever thought, and a lot sooner than anyone would have guessed.

Elizabeth Frye didn't waste time guessing. She had an instinct about these things. Johnny Drummond kept to himself, but when Elizabeth Frye set her cap, it was plain to everyone in town what her intentions were. Now, John was always polite to Elizabeth when they met. What he

thought was hard to tell. A private man, John found himself the object of town jokers and gossips, some light-
hearted, some not. If it made John uncomfortable, it made
Elizabeth furious. She didn't mind being talked about.
Being laughed at was something else again. But no one
ever saw a sign of fury in the cool ice of Elizabeth's eyes,
until one day in the general store.

On this particular winter afternoon, the men were
standing about the general store waiting on their merchan-
dise, or their wives, or just waiting to get warm, when the
door jingled open and Elizabeth entered, just ahead of John
Drummond. She turned and smiled at him, trying to hold
him in conversation with her bright eyes, but John just
tipped his hat—"Good day, Miz Elizabeth"—and went
about his business, leaving Elizabeth to go about hers. She
disappeared into the back of the store.

Well, you know how people sometimes are—out of
sight, out of mind—and it wasn't long before the laughing men standing around the doorway were teasing the
daylights out of John. His friend Tom told him he might
as well give up, because when a woman was as determined to marry as Elizabeth Frye, well . . .

The joking men caught sight of Elizabeth coming to
the front of the store and fell still, just when John
thought he should finally speak up. Into a pool of silence
his words dropped like stones.

"I'll marry Elizabeth Frye when she brings me strawberries in December," he said.

There was a clearing of throats and a shuffling of feet.
Someone pointed with his chin, and Johnny Drummond
turned to find himself caught in the blank shining mirrors
of Elizabeth's eyes. He tried to stammer an apology, but

she only smiled and said softly, "So it's strawberries you want, is it, Mr. Drummond?" and she walked past them all, hair crackling and color high, out the door and into the snow.

Johnny Drummond was a worried man when he left the general store. If anyone had asked him the color of Elizabeth's eyes at that moment, he could have told them—gray and cold and frozen deep.

The next day was Sunday. John, as was his habit, took his mother's silver cup and walked outside to the well. The frost crunched beneath his boots. He pulled the bucket from the well, broke the ice on the surface, and filled his cup. As he began to drink, his eye was caught by a flash of light like sun on yellow roses.

Coming out of the woods was a cat. Tawny gold in the morning light, it strolled up to John. He bent to stroke its head. A chill wind roared in his ears, and the hair lifted on his neck, his back, his arms. In the cat's mouth was a fresh, green stem and two bright, red strawberries. John tried to move. The smell of that ripe fruit filled his nose and throat as he stared down into the eyes of that cat— gray eyes, the color of ice frozen over dark water. The cat began to rub against his legs. It was purring low in its throat, stretching its two front paws up toward John's leg.

John felt those sharp claws in the flesh of his thigh and was shocked into movement. He raised his right hand, still holding the silver cup, and with all the force his frozen will could muster, brought it down on the head of that cat. The cat fell away from him with a snarl, and John ran for the house. He slammed the door behind him and locked it. All the while, logic told him he was acting like a fool. The fear in his heart pounded in his chest and behind his eyes.

His brother had to pry the silver cup from his fingers and sit him by the fire.

On Monday afternoon, John's friend Tom came to call, with an invitation to dinner and some news from town. It seemed Elizabeth Frye hadn't been seen since Saturday afternoon in the general store. No one saw her Sunday, either, and when Monday morning came with still no sign of her, her landlord and his wife got worried. Fearing Elizabeth had become ill, they went to her room. At the door they knocked, waited, and listened. When there was no response, the landlord used his pass key. The way her body lay told them she was dead, even before they saw her head.

The bruise and the blood explained it. She must have tripped and fallen in the dark. That part wasn't so strange. Accidents happen. The strange part was that clutched in Elizabeth's hand was a fresh, green stem with two bright, red strawberries, and the smell of that crushed, ripe fruit hung heavy in the air.

Two things changed about Johnny Drummond after that winter. One thing everyone noticed. John began going to church on Sunday with his brother. They even went to church suppers once a month. Nobody noticed the second thing much. After all, Johnny Drummond was a hard-working man who kept to himself. But John's brother noticed. He couldn't help it. Because the following spring it was the two of them that tore out the strawberry plants by the back fence and planted blackberries there instead.

TWO
Rosie Hopewell

Now, I don't know what you heard, but Jesse Hopewell was the meanest son of a . . . He was the meanest trash on the whole mountain. You got to understand that right off. A man that would use his wife until she was all used up and then try and start on the daughter, well, my pa used to say men like that don't deserve to live. Now, I'm not excusing what happened, mind; I'm just saying that some folks thought that what really happened to Jesse Hopewell was that God had finally paid attention to all the misery he caused.

It all started when the new teacher gave Rosie the smokey gray kitten. Rosie was Jesse's fourteen-year-old daughter, his only child and only kin so far as anyone around these parts knew. Well, the fella didn't mean any harm. He wasn't from around here, and he didn't think anything of giving Rosie the kitten except that it was pretty, and she was pretty, and she wanted it. So Rosie took it on home. She told me later that Jesse came in after spending the day with his whiskey bottle. Everybody knew he was mean sober, but drunk—bless me! He was a coward, though. Not even whiskey made him brave. He always picked on someone who couldn't or wouldn't fight back, so who else but Rosie? Better yet, that poor dumb kitten. Better yet, both of them. I'm telling you, the man had the devil in him. He took that pretty, smoke-soft little thing and dropped it down the well, right in front of Rosie's eyes.

"Don't look at me like that, missy. I did it for your own good. You want folks to talk?"

"I hate you," she whispered. "You kill everything pretty. You killed my mother."

She knew by the look on his face that she was in for it. He caught her by the hair, but she pulled free and ran for the woods. She could hear him swearing behind her.

"I'll get ya! I'll sic the dog on ya! You just see!"

He would never catch her in the woods. She knew more about them in her little finger than he did in his whole body. Besides, he was too drunk. Everybody knew Jesse's habits. He'd drink himself through all of a day and night and then sleep for a whole day, and we'd all get some peace—till he was mean with a hangover, anyway.

Well, now, the gossip says that Rosie ran straight to Old Oak Clearing and sat herself down, her back against the oldest tree. Rosie knew the tree was old, but she didn't know how old. She'd have been surprised at how many people knew where the clearing and the old oak were; there'd been a lot of souls who'd found themselves resting with their backs against that old tree after a run through these woods.

And this is where the gossip really comes in. Of course, it was all hindsight, just because one of the Dynan boys saw Rosie come out of the woods near the clearing and guessed where she'd been.

But, anyway, they say that leaning with her back against that tree, Rosie swore an oath to the devil. They say that the devil himself gave her the power to witch Jesse, and in exchange for that power, she gave him her immortal soul. The Dynan boy said he saw Rosie come out of the woods. It was night, and there was no moon, but he could tell that Rosie could see quite clearly in the dark.

Now, do you believe that? I mean, if it was a dark night with no moon, how could he tell anything? And even if you could make a pact with the devil—and I'm not saying that you can't—why in the world would any-one think that Jesse Hopewell was worth their immortal soul? Rosie was young, but she wasn't stupid. Mostly she took after her mother's side and was genuinely sweet in spite of her daddy. There were some folks who said that at least Rosie had time on her side. She'd probably out-live Jesse, the evil old thing. Sell her soul, indeed. People think selling your soul is something full of brimstone and lightning. Well, there are other ways to lose your soul. Doing nothing when you know you should do some-thing, that's one way. I mean, everybody knew what was going on in that house.

In a place like this, everyone is in everyone else's pocket, so we all knew the next day what had happened when Rosie got home from the woods. Jesse could barely stand, he was so drunk. He got up swearing, and she stared him down. People say something happened to her in the woods, but I say something happened to her when her father dropped that kitten down that well. It was bound to come out sooner or later. Rosie was her moth-er's daughter, but I was her mother's sister, and blood will tell. She was fourteen going on fifteen, righteous with youth and passionate mad. And Jesse was a coward.

"Get yourself out of my way, and don't you ever raise a hand to me again, ever," she said.

When Jesse was on his whiskey run the next morning,

he told folks in town that he was gonna put her out. After the way she looked at him, well, she wasn't gonna put the evil eye on him. He had heard her, he said. She'd kept him awake all night, moving things around in the firelight and talking to herself. Why, even his old dog wouldn't stay in the house with her.

Probably the old dog wouldn't stay in the house because Rosie was busy cleaning it. She told me she'd been so mad, she couldn't sleep, and so she worked through the night. I hadn't seen the place swept so clean, not since my sister, Rosie's mama, died.

Jesse gave a snort when he came in. He looked around. "Think you're mighty fancy, dontcha?" he said.

Jesse was only mad because it was harder to get drunk in a room that looked like decent folk lived there. Rosie kept working. The smell of ammonia and lemon soap filled the air, forcing Jesse outdoors. His old dog lay crouched just outside the gate. Jesse walked across the yard and sat down with his back against the fence post. He pulled his whiskey bottle out of his pocket, drank, and watched his daughter work. Rosie swept the porch, stacked the garbage to be burned, and tugged a bucket of fresh water into the house.

The town gossips pieced it together later from what the teacher told the shopkeeper in Horner's General Store. The teacher said when he came by on his way to town that evening, Jesse was on his feet, leaning against the fence post. He was trying to coax the dog into the yard, but he wasn't having any luck.

The teacher told the shopkeeper that when he said "Good evening" to Jesse, Jesse opened his mouth to answer, then left it hanging open, staring over the teacher's shoulder as if he'd seen a ghost. The teacher thought he was having a fit, until, turning around, he saw her, too. Rosie, standing on the porch, her dark hair soft on her slender neck, her dark eyes glowing in her pale face. She was just like her mama, beautiful and sweet.

Later, when the teacher talked of the night he saw Rosie, *really* saw her, he talked about looking back and seeing her in the swiftly darkening air, a slender porch figure lifting a pale white hand. It was while looking back at Rosie that he saw Jesse Hopewell shoulder his rifle and heard him whistle for his dog. Man and dog set out up the mountain, and the night woods closed over them.

Rosie didn't worry when Jesse didn't come home that night. He didn't come home a lot of nights. The morning dawned lazy and bright. The littlest Dynan boy said Rosie was sitting in the kitchen when he knocked frantically on the door.

"Rosie! Rosie!" He could see her through the screen door. "There's been an accident, Rosie! My ma says to come right away! Your pa was killed in the night. One of them mountain cats, my pa says. A big one. Pa says old Jess was killed before he could even lift his rifle. Tore up the dog, too. Pa says they're making up a posse to go after the cat. Ain't been one around here in years, Ma says. Ma says come stay with us."

When he told his brothers about it later, his eyes were big with excitement.

"You tell your mama 'thank you,'" Rosie said, "but I'll stay here. I'm not afraid to be alone."

"Ain't you comin' to claim the body?" asked the boy.

"No," said Rosie.

She turned away from the door, then, leaving the bewildered boy on the porch looking through the screen. He says Rosie went back to her chair and picked up a cup. As she sipped her tea, a big smokey gray cat jumped into her lap, and she stroked it gently and slowly, from the tip of its smokey nose to the tip of its smokey tail.

Now there are some folks around here who'll tell you that it was the kitten the teacher gave her come back as a grown cat to do her bidding, just because old Jesse got himself killed by a wildcat. I don't think the teacher heard the rumors, or if he did, he didn't pay them any mind. The worst of them stopped after he and Rosie were married, anyway.

Honestly, who could blame her for not claiming the body? She couldn't afford to bury it, and why should she go into debt for that mean-hearted, miserable old man? Well, don't look at me; I certainly wasn't going to pay for it. Oh, I made sure the town buried him. Listen, Jesse Hopewell was one of those men that no one, and I mean no one, not even the man he bought his liquor from, was going to miss. I buried what was left of the dog myself. Poor old thing. He couldn't desert even a no-good sinner like Jesse in the end. But he never should have gotten between Jesse and that cat.

The big gray cat the Dynan boy saw was only visiting in the Hopewell house; it didn't stay long. Rosie took to raising babies and a garden that put the rest of us to shame. The rumors died almost altogether then. Of course, I always knew it wasn't true. That Rosie hexed her daddy with a vengeful kitten come back from a watery grave? It was downright ridiculous. All right, I'll grant you, people tell stories about a smokey gray cat that's more than a cat prowling around these hills, and I'll even grant you some of those stories might be true. But a drowned kitten is a drowned kitten, and those stories were around long before Rosie. Oh, I know what you're thinking. What about that big gray cat the little Dynan boy saw? As if there were only one gray cat on this whole mountain. It just goes to show you that you shouldn't be jumping to conclusions. Besides, that big gray cat the Dynan boy saw with Rosie? That wasn't Rosie's cat. It was mine.

THREE
Skulls and Bones, Ghosts and Gold

Part I

Jack Blacksea named his daughters Ruby and Pearl because they were his only jewels. Ruby taught school in the one-room schoolhouse. Pearl hired out as domestic help and had worked for several of the big county families, but mostly for the Sutton-Sherwoods, the first family of Vidalia.

See, there used to be the Suttons, and there used to be the Sherwoods, and there was a long line of Sutton-Sherwood alliances, some good, some bad, all expected by both families; and when Ransome Robert Sutton met Lavinia Chevalier Sherwood, they . . . well, they weren't oil and water so much as they were fire and powder, if you get my drift.

Ransome Robert Sutton—they called him "Handsome Ransome" because he was such a devil with the women—well, Ransome was a good-natured, somewhat wild boy, and he married well when he married Lavinia Sherwood. He married very well. Some people might even say he had married above himself—especially his wife, especially when she decided she just couldn't tolerate being under the same roof with him and set up her own place, but that wasn't until after their son, Daniel, was born. Anyway, Ransome was good-natured, as I said, and he enjoyed the company of his friends, gambling at dice or horses, and visiting with his son, Daniel—at least, after the boy was grown and could hunt and play cards.

It was the Sutton-Sherwoods that Pearl Blacksea came to work for exclusively—the Ransome Sutton-Sherwoods, not the Lavinia Chevalier Sutton-Sherwoods—and Pearl pretty much held the place together, managing the house, handling the household money, making sure there was enough feed to get the livestock through the winter.

Ransome Sutton-Sherwood respected Pearl. She had a strong right arm, as he found out the one and only time he tried to get familiar, and she was a good shot. He admired Pearl, too. She was cool, calm, and kind. She kept his house and stable running smooth as cream, and for this he paid her handsomely, some might even say too handsomely, especially if they were busy sticking their noses where they didn't belong. On her side, Pearl tolerated Ransome. She liked his house, had a good head for figures, knew how to jolly the stable boys into doing their jobs, and on the whole did only half again as much work as she got paid for. It was a matter of pride, really. She used to tell her sister Ruby that no matter what fool thing Ransome Sutton-Sherwood asked her to do, she had never yet failed to do it: "Foolish requests from a foolish man have to be taken seriously when he's paying the bills," she always said.

It has to be admitted, Pearl did have a reputation for not suffering fools gladly, or even patiently, and one fool she didn't have a lightning second for was Rusty Rittendover. He was one of Ransome's card-playing buddies, and he was always giving Pearl more grief than he was worth. Once he even bet Ransome fifty dollars that Pearl would be too scared to go out at midnight and fetch a bottle of whiskey, then got mad 'cause he had to pay up when Ransome—well, Pearl, really—won the bet. Ever since then Rusty'd been hatching a plot to spook Pearl witless and have her come screaming for help with as many witnesses as he could manage.

One late night the Sutton-Sherwood card room was filled with men's bragging, bets, and cigar smoke. Rusty leaned back on two legs of his chair and said to Ransome, "I bet I know something your Pearl can't do."

Ransome laughed. "What's the matter, Rusty? Got too much money?"

"You're thinking about that old bet, but a walk down a moonlit road at midnight is nothing compared to this," said Rusty. "I'll bet you another fifty dollars that Pearl can't go to the boneyard at midnight and fetch us back a skull."

"If a bottle of whiskey is worth fifty dollars, a skull ought to be worth at least a hundred," said Pearl quietly from the doorway.

"A hundred it is, then!" Rusty slammed the table with his open palm, a wicked gleam in his eye.

Pearl gave the drunken men a look they didn't appreciate and out she swept, headed for the graveyard and whatever mischief Rusty had cooked up. And he had been cooking. In the graveyard, behind the simple stone markers of less showy grief, stood the elaborately carved, if ill-kept, Sutton-Sherwood family mausoleum. Inside that mausoleum, hidden behind broken stones and piles of bones, was Rusty's best and maybe only real friend, James Lance Pertrell. James Lance was supposed to scare Pearl, but moonlit mausoleums not being quite his cup of

24

tea, he wasn't too far from scared himself. He was mighty relieved when the wrought-iron gate creaked open under Pearl's hand, and she walked into the cemetery.

Pearl picked her way carefully over the sunken stones to the Sutton-Sherwood mausoleum, it being the likeliest place for bones. That mausoleum was the ugliest piece of eternal real estate she'd ever set eyes on. The gate was wide open, and she walked in. Ah, there were a lot of Sutton-Sherwoods littering the stone shelves, little piles of the first-family-of-Vidalia ancestors gathering dust. Pearl picked up the closest skull. It looked like it belonged to Great-Great-Uncle Walter Sherwood.

"Put that down," moaned James Lance. "That's the skull of my beloved father."

Pearl put it down. "Wouldn't want to deprive you of your father's company," she said blandly. She picked up a second skull, this time from the pile marked "Elizabeth Rutledge Smythe-Sutton."

"Leave that!" moaned the voice again. "It's my beloved mother."

"Apparently she wasn't married to your beloved father." Pearl sniffed. She walked around the shelves and stopped in front of the oldest pile, picking up the skull of the first Roger Sherwood, great-great-great-granddaddy of them all.

"Put that down," moaned the voice. "That's the skull of my—"

"I know who it is," said Pearl. "And I'm taking him nonetheless. Like as not, his great-great-great-grandson will bring him back after he's won his hundred dollars." And Pearl wrapped the skull in her apron and slipped out of the mausoleum, closing and locking the gate behind her.

As she walked down the road toward the Sutton-

Sherwood main house, she heard the mausoleum spook howl behind her like a banshee.

When she swept into the card room, the sudden light made her blink. Rusty sat up suddenly, his mouth open, and Ransome said, "Welcome back, Pearl. Have I won a hundred dollars?"

In answer Pearl lay the skull in the center of the table, amid the cards, the coins, and the crumpled bills. Then she smiled at Rusty Rittendover and said to them all, "I'm going up now. Don't bother me with any more foolishness tonight, if you please." She turned toward the stairs, and over the laughter of the other players heard Rusty holler, "Wait . . . stop! Didn't you hear anything while you were in the graveyard?"

"Well, yes," said Pearl. "An old relative of the family, didn't want me taking anyone, but I promised that Mr. Ransome would bring back the skull as soon as you were finished playing cards. That didn't seem to help much. He was howling fit to wake the dead when I left."

Ransome fell out of his chair laughing as Rusty Rittendover raced out of the card room and down the moonlit road to the cemetery. James Lance was never quite the same after that night. He wasn't quite up to snuff before that night, either, so I'm not sure it really made that much difference. James wasn't quite so willing to go along with Rusty's shenanigans after that, though.

The story of Pearl's adventure in the Sutton-Sherwood mausoleum was the talk of the town. James Lance Pertrell's mother was sorely grieved at Rusty Rittendover leaving her son alone in the Sutton-Sherwood boneyard, and she made no bones about her displeasure. Rusty finally gave up trying to get the better of Pearl; it cost him too much money.

Part II

It was shortly after Pearl's unexpected adventure in the boneyard that Daniel Sutton-Sherwood, the only son of Ransome Sutton-Sherwood and Lavinia Chevalier Sutton-Sherwood, rode up to his father's house.

Daniel had been having a few problems with his mother, the late dear departed Lavinia Sutton-Sherwood. He had managed to avoid trouble with his mother while she was alive by not being at home; tours of Europe, business in Chicago, the occasional trip to New York City or New Orleans kept him in constant motion and just barely out of his mother's loving but strangling reach. When Lavinia died, she left everything to Daniel; after all, he'd been a dutiful, if not always attentive, son. Daniel moved into her house and prepared to take his expected place among the county gentry, his first official act being the arrangements for his mother's elaborate funeral. Lavinia Chevalier Sutton-Sherwood was laid to rest with a spectacular number of roses, hymns, and speeches, and the entire county was witness to it.

But Daniel had been seeing a lot more of his mother since her death than he had while she was living. In fact, she came to dinner every night . . . and lunch . . . and breakfast. Daniel was at his wit's end. He couldn't keep a servant on the place. He was a fine hand at gentling horses, but he couldn't cook worth a damn, and he was getting tired of eating canned beans and hardtack. He was to the point where the rules of fair play meant nothing to him if he could get a good meal, and he offered Pearl twice as much as his daddy was paying her to come and work for him.

Well, if the story of Pearl and the boneyard was all over the county in a day, you can be sure that Pearl knew all about Daniel Sutton-Sherwood's travails with his restless, dearly-but-not-entirely-departed mother. Pearl's sister, Ruby, had come over to visit, and she was there when Daniel made his offer.

Ruby raised an eyebrow. "Just why would you be paying Pearl so much to do what she does here already for less?" she asked.

Daniel was a bit distracted by Ruby's eyes, so it took him a minute to answer.

"Oh, well, you won't believe it, Miss Ruby, but it's Lavinia, my mother. She may be passed away but she isn't passed on. She's driven everybody but me out of the main house. I can barely keep the stable hands on, and even they won't come up to the house after dark. I can't say that I blame them. I'm tempted to sleep in the barn myself. Mother has the most disconcerting habit of appearing without a sound and then howling in your ear. The cat's gone bald, water won't boil, and even the clocks have stopped keeping good time. I'm a desperate man, Miss Ruby."

Then he smiled. He had a fine smile, that Daniel did, and there were many women from New Orleans to Chicago who could testify to it.

The usually imperturbable Ruby was charmed by that smile. Pearl, on the other hand, was charmed by the truth, and the money, and the fact that Ruby was charmed for the first time in her life. Pearl took the job right there. She packed up and rode off in the carriage her new employer had sent, despite the entreaties of his father.

Daniel Sutton-Sherwood lived in what had been the architectural signature statement of Lavinia Chevalier Sutton-Sherwood. For such a seemingly pretentious woman, it was a remarkably unpretentious residence. It was a rambling old house, with orchards and a rose garden and a wraparound porch with climbing clematis and morning glories. The stables were spic and span, the meadows glorious with bluebells and clover, and the sweet smell of blooming lilacs was everywhere. A scene further from a haunting you could not find, not even if you spent a summer of Sundays searching for it.

But haunted it was, and Pearl knew it. Ruby knew it, too, and she came after school to offer her moral support. Oh, all right, she came because she was dying, if you'll pardon the expression, of curiosity. Daniel made excuses to frequent the kitchen, and while Ruby and Pearl made dinner he got underfoot with alarming frequency. Pearl carefully set the dining room table with a lace cloth, good china, candles, and place settings for two. Daniel sat at one end of the long table.

"Who's the second place for?" he asked.

Pearl answered him like a sister.

"Don't be dense, Daniel. That is the place for your mother, the lady of the house, and I do believe this is her now."

It is a given that both Pearl and Ruby were brave girls, but neither was quite certain what material form the maternal apparition would take. Lavinia Chevalier Sutton-Sherwood made quite an entrance. She materialized at the head of the table in a cyclone of light and fog, her beringed hand on the back of the high-backed chair, her silk burial dress uncreased, her lace cuffs starched. In a voice that pierced the veil between life and death and made Daniel's ears hurt, she demanded, "Who dares to sit at my table?"

"Mother, please, is such drama really necessary?" inquired her exasperated son.

Pearl interrupted quickly.

"This place is for the lady of the house, ma'am. Won't you sit down?"

The dear departed's eyes went from baleful to delighted in the space of a heartbeat.

"Thank you, my dear," said Lavinia. She looked meaningfully at her son. "At least someone in this house knows how to be polite." And with a ruffle of lace tablecloth, she was gone.

Daniel stared.

"Is it over?" he asked, daring to hope for the first time in weeks.

"Oh, not likely," said Pearl. "But at least now you can eat."

After dinner, Pearl cleared and left Ruby to tour the rose gardens with Daniel.

In the morning, Pearl set the table for breakfast, two places, one for Daniel and one for Lavinia, who appeared, nodded approvingly at the breakfast flowers, and departed. Luncheon was much the same, with a brief appearance from a gracious, nodding Lavinia.

Daniel was flabbergasted but happy. He took his bemusement to town to visit Ruby, and then up to the county seat on overnight business.

That evening Pearl set the table, and Lavinia made her expected luminous appearance. But her expected disappearance did not occur.

"Pearl," she asked, "aren't you afraid of me?"

"With all due respect, ma'am, is there any reason I should be?" Pearl replied. "You are dead, if not gone, after all."

Lavinia smiled, and for a moment Pearl could see how Daniel's daddy Ransome must have fallen in love with that smile.

"Come down to the cellar with me, Pearl," said Lavinia. "We'll take care of a bit of unfinished business, and then I will be well and truly gone."

Pearl dried her hands on her apron and followed the glowing figure down the dark stairs. Lavinia pointed to a brick turned differently from the others, and when Pearl pushed it, a section of the wall opened, revealing a hidden cupboard. Inside were two large bags of gold.

"There now," said a fading Lavinia. "That gold came from my mother to me, and from her mother to her, and now I give it to you. I was always afraid Ransome would gamble everything away, so I put it here for safekeeping. Tell my son one bag is for his bride on their wedding day, and one bag is for you, because you are a gracious, well-brought up young woman who knows the proper way to behave, even with the strain of unexpected company."

All that remained of Lavinia was a pale glow that lit Pearl's way up the stairs, and then that, too, was gone.

Pearl stayed long enough to see Ruby and Daniel happily married; then she packed her bags with some of Lavinia's gold and lit out for the Great Northwest. Having exhausted the unexpected in Vidalia, she went where the unexpected was more likely to be found. After all, she had grace with the unexpected. Daniel's mother told her so.

FOUR
The Severed Hand

Fair Mary was merry, Fair Mary was kind. She had more brothers than you can count on one hand, for she had seven. Her brothers had raised her from a babe, for their parents had died when she was very young. A fine job they'd done of it, too, for there were many young men who wanted to marry Mary. The blacksmith's son, the minister's nephew, the butcher's boy—they came courting every Sunday and sat in the parlor, trying their country best to charm her. But Mary was not interested in any of these young men. She had known them all her life, and, if the truth be told, they bored her to distraction. She longed to meet a man unlike any other she had met before, someone mysterious and exciting. And you know what they say. Be careful what you wish for.

One day there came to town a man unlike any other Mary had ever met. He was tall and straight, with bright green eyes and shocking red hair. His clothes were elegant, and his manner even more so. His name was Mr. Fox, and soon, very soon, he began courting Mary. He would come by on Sunday and sit in the parlor and tell her stories of his travels, of all the exotic places he had been, and the strange and unusual sights he had seen. It wasn't long before the other young men stopped coming, for it was clear Mary had made her choice. The engagement was soon announced, to the chagrin of the country suitors, and to the delight of the headstrong Mary.

Now, Mr. Fox spoke to Mary of his manor house on the other side of the woods, filled with the curious and beautiful things collected on his travels. "You must come and see the house, my Mary," he would say. "For soon you will be mistress there." But although they spoke often of such a visit, somehow it was never arranged.

One Saturday Mary was walking through the woods, and, what with thinking of this and thinking of that, she wandered deeper into the woods than she ever had ventured before. The light was fading, but she was not frightened, not then. She knew that if she stayed on the path, it would curve back to meet the road, and she would easily find her way home, daylight or no, so she continued on. Soon she came to a clearing, and on the edge of the clearing was a great house. She knew it was the home of Mr. Fox, for he had described it to her. "Well then, this is good fortune," she thought. "I will knock on the door, and Mr. Fox will give me something cool to drink, and perhaps a ride back to town." Across the fragrant meadow she went, and up the great front steps to the great front door. Raising her hand to knock, Mary looked up. Carved above the great front door were the words "Be bold. Be bold."

She did not know what it meant. "A family motto," thought Mary. "I must gain its meaning from my Mr. Fox." Being bold enough, she knocked on the door. The sound of her knocking echoed inside the house, echoed on and back, but no one came. "Now this is strange," Mary thought, "for in a house this large, there should be many servants." She knocked again, and again there was no answer, and thinking only to herself, "Oh, Mr. Fox, he would not mind," Mary turned the golden doorknob until the door opened smoothly beneath her hand.

She stepped into a great hall that fairly took her breath. Beneath her feet was a marble floor polished to mirror brightness. Above her head was a crystal chandelier that glittered in the afternoon sun, and curving up to the second floor was a long stairway, wide and graceful. Mary looked at the elegant stairway and imagined herself sweeping down the stairs, her stairs, on the arm of Mr. Fox, her Mr. Fox, making a grand entrance into the grand hall. Thinking only to herself, "Oh, Mr. Fox, he would not mind," Mary ran lightly up the stairs, intending only to sweep down them again. But at the top of the stairs there was another door and carved above the door were the words "Be bold. Be bold. But not too bold." She did not know what they meant, but nevertheless, she was bold enough.

She opened the second door and stepped into the most richly appointed bedroom she had ever seen. The walls hung with tapestries embroidered in gold, the bed was covered with velvet, the floor with carpets in colors that glowed like fire. And across the room, there was yet another door, a third door, a closet door.

Now, closets in those days were not like closets today, but more like small rooms. A person could step inside them, the clothes hanging about the walls. Mary thought of the elegant clothes Mr. Fox always wore, never the same twice since she had known him, and wondered if there was room in that closet for her clothes. Thinking only to herself , "Oh, Mr. Fox, he would not mind," she crossed the room. Carved above the closet door were the words "Be bold. Be bold. But not too bold. Lest your heart's blood run cold." Mary did not know what the words meant, but she did not let that stop her. Mary opened the door and stepped inside.

It took a few moments for her eyes to adjust to darkness. When they had, she saw before her three great cauldrons, huge iron pots. She stepped up to the first and saw that it was full of human hair. Red, gold, black, and brown gleamed in the shadowy light. Her heart began to beat a little faster. Mary stepped to the second cauldron and saw that it was filled with human bones. She knew they were human bones; she could tell by the skulls gleaming there in the half-light, and her heart beat faster still. Mary stepped to the third cauldron and saw that it was full of some dark liquid. She dipped her fingertips into the liquid, smelled it, and knew that it was blood.

Heart in her throat, Mary backed up against the closet wall. She thought she would be sick. Hands over her mouth to keep from screaming, she ran from the closet, slamming the door behind her.

Across the bedroom she ran, slamming that door behind her, too. She started down the great curving stair. And that was when she saw him. Through the front window she saw him, Mr. Fox, coming across the meadow, dragging a young woman behind him. Mary was trapped there on the stairs. She could not go up. She could not go out. She ran down the long curved stairway and hid in the shadows beneath it.

The great front door flew open, and Mr. Fox entered, dragging the young woman across the gleaming marble floor. He pulled her up the stairs. In a last desperate effort to save herself, the young woman reached out and grabbed hold of the banister, and Mr. Fox, without missing a beat, drew his sword and cut off her hand. The hand flew threw the air and landed in Mary's lap, where she crouched hidden beneath the stair. She knew her life was

forfeit if he discovered her. Mary heard the bedroom door open and close, then the closet door, then silence. She wrapped the severed hand in her apron and ran from Mr. Fox's lair. She ran across the meadow. She ran through the woods. She did not stop running until she reached the safety of her brothers' house.

The next day was Sunday, and as was his habit, Mr. Fox came to visit Mary. They sat in the parlor, Mary's back to the heavy drapes that shut out the wind and weather, and although Mr. Fox's stories were as witty as ever, she was strangely silent.

Finally, Mr. Fox said to her, "Mary, my dear, what is it? You do not seem yourself today."

And Mary replied, "Oh, Mr. Fox, last night I had a dream."

"A dream?" said Mr. Fox. "I am very good at interpreting dreams. You tell me what you dreamt, and I will tell you what it meant."

And so Mary began.

"I dreamed I was walking through the woods, and I came to a great clearing. On the edge of the clearing was a great house, and carved above the great front door were the words 'Be bold. Be bold.'"

"But it was not so," said Mr. Fox.

"In my dream, sir, in my dream it was so. In my dream I opened the great front door and went into a great hall. Up a curving stair there was a second door and carved above it were the words 'Be bold. Be bold. But not too bold.'"

"But it was not so," said Mr. Fox. "And it is not so."

"In my dream, sir, it was so, in my dream. In my dream I opened the second door, and across a rich bedroom was yet a third door, and carved above it the words 'Be bold. Be bold. But not too bold. Lest your heart's blood run cold.' I opened the third door and within found three cauldrons, one full of human hair, one full of human bones, and one full of human blood. I ran from that room, sir, down the stair. And then I saw you, Mr. Fox, I saw you, coming across the meadow, dragging a young woman by the hair. You pulled her up the stair, and when she reached out to save herself, you drew your sword and cut off her hand."

Mr. Fox had gone very pale. "But it was not so!" he cried. "And it is not so. And God forbid that it should be so."

"Ah, but it was so. And it is so. And here is the hand to prove it so." And between them on the table she laid that severed hand.

Mr. Fox stood so quickly his chair fell over behind him. His green green eyes glittered in his pale pale face, and his hand was on his sword. In a deadly whisper he said, "Ah, it was so. And it is so, but you are the only one who knows, and you will never tell."

Mary stood and threw open the drapes behind her. Her seven brothers fell on Mr. Fox, and, dragging him to the back of the house, they did to him there what he had done to so many others.

FIVE
Rubies

Oh, the seduction had been so smooth. It happened right beneath their noses, in front of their eyes, and none of them ever saw what he was doing. Rafael, a traveling trovatore, had been visiting the house for months, singing and telling stories. He did not appear to treat Helene differently from the other young women of the household. He sang love songs to all of them, kissed all their hands, admired all their jewels—especially their jewels. He was like a black-eyed raven, unable to resist anything that glittered, though he wore little jewelry himself—one gold ring, set in one pierced ear, like a pirate.

The cousins thought him most romantic, but it was the daughters of the house who mattered. There were two—Giovanna was the elder; Helene, the younger. Both sisters had their choice of sparkling gems to adorn their olive skin and dark hair, but even the costliest gems paled against Helene's beauty. Only her mother's rubies did her justice. There were bracelets, and earrings, and dozens of hairpins replete with shimmering stones. But the necklace dazzled the eye—three strands of perfect rubies set in gold. The rubies sat like drops of blood on Helene's hair and throat, and they glittered when she laughed, as if they were laughing, too.

Afterward, Giovanna blamed herself.

"Oh, why did I not see it?" she cried. "I should have

seen it. I was close to her, loved her. I should have known. I should have known."

But no one had known. There had been a terrible storm that night. The wind howled inland from over the sea, and the lightning cracked across the cliffs. Giovanna, awakened by the fury of the storm, had discovered Helene's empty bed and the empty jewel case. She roused the house. When they found Rafael's bed unslept in, they thought the two had run away together. The brothers were on their way to the stables when Rafael's riderless horse galloped into the courtyard. Rafael staggered in behind and fell to his knees on the cobblestones. The strong arms of the waiting brothers pulled him to his feet. He clung to them desperately, trying to catch his breath to speak.

"I tried to stop them. . . . Helene and her lover. . . . I chased after them, they were on the cliffside road, heading for the harbor, but before I reached them . . . the lightning. . . . Helene's horse ran away with her, toward the cliffs . . . they went over, Helene and her horse, both of them went over. I caught him, the man, but I slipped in the mud, and he fled on his horse. I tried to chase him, but my horse threw me, and he got away."

They could see Rafael was badly hurt. His clothes were muddy and torn, his face bruised, one eye blackened. His gold hoop had been pulled from his ear, and the torn flesh bled down the side of his face and neck. His story rang with truth; he was weeping as he told it.

"Forgive me. Forgive me. I was too late. I was too late."

He sobbed in Giovanna's arms. The family, in their own sorrow, tried to comfort him.

The brothers' search for Helene's lover was futile. They did not even know who they were looking for.

Giovanna was sick with grief. She went to her room and discovered what she had missed before—a letter from Helene and their mother's rubies. "My dear sister," the letter said. "By the time you read this, I will be far at sea with my true love. I thought to use mother's rubies to finance our new life, but found I could not. They belong here with you, in the house where she was born. Please forgive me. Father would never permit this union. I am so happy. Love, Helene." Giovanna wept until she could weep no more.

The rain stopped. The wind changed. Giovanna sat at the window, her head on her arms. She was half-drunk with tears when she heard the whisper from the sea. "Giovanna. . ."

She thought she was mad, but then she heard it again, "Giovanna. Giovanna."

She put on a cloak and went out into the night. She walked the long dark road to the cliffs; the moon, buried in cloud, struggled to light the sky. Giovanna stared into the freezing water at the place where Helene had fallen. From behind her a familiar voice moaned, "Giovanna."

Helene took form from the mist and the moonlight, but only the moonlight put life into her eyes. She was battered and bruised. Her dark hair was darker with blood, and her shift was torn. Her face, her beautiful face, was pale and swollen, and the water ran from her hair, from her fingers, from her eyes, as if it had no end.

"Helene," Giovanna moaned. "Helene, who was it? Who did this to you?"

Helene held out her hand. In her palm was one gold ring, a golden hoop fit for a pirate's ear.

"Avenge me," whispered Helene.

Giovanna stared past her murdered sister. Behind

Helene were the shades of other women, with bodies of mist and eyes without light. Helene was not the only one. There had been others. Dawn was brightening the sky when Giovanna walked back to the house, Helene's whisper still in her ear: "Sister, avenge me. Avenge us all."

Helene's body was never recovered, but the funeral mass was held nonetheless. At the service, Rafael had the eyes of a grieving angel. The young cousins found the trovatore romantically tragic. It was all Giovanna could do not to accuse him right there in the church. Despite the family's hospitable urging, Rafael left immediately after the services, but not before Giovanna obtained his promise to return. It was easy enough. Rafael had seen the necklace around her neck, the rubies she wore as her legacy from Helene. Being the thieving raven she knew he was, she trusted he would come back for them, and a few weeks later, he did.

They met in secret on his return, like trysting lovers. He saw Giovanna as desirable now, she made sure of it, sighing about her loneliness, the rubies warm against her skin. It was a simple matter to bring him to his knees. Rafael chose his moment well—twilight in the rose garden, among the scent of sea and blossoms. He had always loved Giovanna as a sister, he claimed, but now he had come to love her as his future wife. Giovanna demurred, at first, but let him persuade her with promises and poetry.

"I do love you, Rafael," she lied, "but my father would never permit this marriage. Our only hope is to run away together."

He was kneeling before her, his head bent over her hands, hiding a sudden smile.

"Giovanna, my own, do we not have the right to some

happiness after such terrible grief? Surely our love is a sign of God's blessing and an answer to my prayers."

Oh, his words were dipped in passion and poison. She told him she would run away with him.

"I will wear as many of my jewels as I can and carry still more, so we will be able to travel far and live well."

"Tonight," said Rafael.

Stone-hearted, Giovanna smiled at him, kissed him, and called him "my love."

In the middle of the night, Giovanna rose from her bed to dress. She did not dress like a lovesick woman running away with her lover but like a priestess preparing for some dark ceremony. She wore jeweled pins in her hair and bracelets from her wrists to her elbows; her dress was covered in tiny gems that flashed in the firelight. Around her neck she wore Helene's rubies, dark as blood. Giovanna pulled her cape up around her throat and pinned it with an emerald brooch the size of her fist; Rafael's eyes gleamed when he saw it.

They rode out of the courtyard, horses' hooves muffled, along the road that led to the harbor and the sea. Rafael stopped when they reached the crossroads leading to the cliff where Helene had fallen. A moment, he asked? A moment to ask Helene's blessing on their marriage? Giovanna could not refuse him. They dismounted and walked to the edge of the cliff, his hand on her elbow. She drew back.

"Not so close," Giovanna said. "It's such a long way down."

Rafael turned and faced her, then, his back to the sea.

"Your sister feared the edge as well, but in the end she

died as easily as the six who came before her, and so will you. But you will not take to the sea what I have waited for all this time."

Giovanna was still, so still.

"Your jewels, lady," he said. "I will have them."

Giovanna undid her cloak, and it slipped to the ground. The sun was coming up over the edge of the sea, and the light caught the rubies around Giovanna's throat and set them on fire. Rafael could not take his eyes from those flaming stones. Giovanna reached behind her head to undo the clasp that held the rubies.

"You want them?" she said. "Catch them." And she tossed the necklace toward the edge of the cliff. With a cry Rafael lunged and snatched them from the air. His gloating did not last long. Giovanna pushed him. He clutched the rubies even as he fell. Rafael was struggling to keep his head above the waves when seven pairs of pale white arms came up out of the sea and took him.

"There," Giovanna said. "Seven brides have you sent to the bottom of the sea, and now you will be bridegroom to them all."

Giovanna picked up her cloak and rode home. That night, and every night after, she had only pleasant dreams.

SIX
Sea Child

When her son, Johnny, drowned, Martha Seton stopped singing. Oh, she was still a loving wife and help-mate, but you could tell her heart wasn't in it. Joe, her husband, hoped she would get over it in time, but Martha just grew quieter and quieter. She never went down to Cliff's End Beach after Johnny died. She avoided the water altogether when she could, but there was no escaping the smell of the sea in her nostrils or the taste of salt on her lips. After a while her silence seemed natural, and everyone but Joe forgot that Martha used to sing the tides in and out.

One summer night, a year after her boy was drowned, Martha lay beside her husband in the dark, listening to the sound of his breathing, the sound of the sea. It was nearly dawn. She heard the muffled clatter of the milk wagon and the clank of Old Spry leaving the new milk can on the porch and picking up the old. Then she heard something else. At first she thought she was dreaming, but listening to Joe snore, she knew she was awake, and she knew the sound. It was a baby crying in the night. The low wail came over and over again. It was enough to break her heart.

"Joe! Joe, wake up!" Martha whispered.

"What? What is it, Martha?"

"Listen. Can't you hear it?"

"What? No, nothing."

Joe heard only the wind and the sea, while to Martha the cry was more and more urgent.

"Joe, are you mad? You must hear it."

"Martha, you've been dreaming again. . . ."

"Am I awake now? Yes? Then I hear a baby crying as clear as if it were in this room. I tell you I hear it." Martha stopped and listened again. "There now, you must hear that."

Joe looked sadly at his wife.

"You don't hear it, do you? The singing? You really don't. There . . . it's stopped now."

"Martha, darling, you must have been asleep, dreaming again. . . ."

Joe sat up with Martha for a while, but soon dropped off. Martha lay awake, listening as the sky grew light, but all she heard was the sound of gulls crying over the sea.

Later that morning, Joe went out for the milk.

"Well, I'm damned," he said, as he came in and swung the milk can onto the table. "Old Spry is getting old or crooked. He's shorted us at least three, four cups of milk today."

"Oh, don't be silly, Joe. Old Spry is no older than you, and a straight limb doesn't grow crooked overnight. Probably the cats got to it before you did, is all."

Joe didn't care what happened to the milk, not really. He'd woke up worried about Martha. The dreams had been terrible the weeks after Johnny's death, but last night had been worse than ever. He was so glad to get such a reasonable response, he didn't care if she was cranky with him. Their day passed in work and meals, and that night when Joe's head touched the pillow, he was sound asleep.

Martha lay awake through the night, waiting. Just before dawn, she heard Old Spry pick up the old milk can and leave the new. When the cry came again, she didn't

wake Joe. She slipped out of bed and down the stairs. She was heading for the door, determined to locate the source of the crying, when a shadow passed by the window. Martha pulled the curtains back in time to see the figure of a woman walking in the fog toward Cliff's End. The woman walked slowly, holding something in her hands. Martha ran to unlock the cottage door. The crying would break her heart.

"Martha! Are you walking in your sleep? What are you doing?" Joe asked, coming down the stairs.

"I've seen her, Joe. I've seen her!" Martha flung open the door. "There! There, do you see her?"

Joe peered anxiously at his wife.

"Don't look at me, Joe. Look there. There!"

Joe looked, but where Martha saw the figure of a young woman fading into the morning fog, Joe saw nothing.

"Come back to bed, Martha, you'll catch a chill," Joe said gently.

Martha looked at him and sighed. It was no use. He didn't see, he didn't hear, and maybe she was mad, after all.

"No, no, Joe, I won't go to bed. I won't sleep, anyway. It'll be light soon. I'll go into the kitchen and make some tea."

And that's just what she did, leaving Joe worrying by the door. He was so worried about her, that later that morning he didn't mention that Old Spry had shorted them four cups of milk again.

The days passed, as days will, and Martha stayed busy, but silent. At lunch when Joe came home from his boat, he found her on the porch, frowning toward Cliff's End.

That night even Joe slept lightly, but not lightly

enough. Martha waited until she heard the milk cans clink and Old Spry drive away in the milk wagon. When the crying began again, she was ready. Standing by the open cottage door, Martha saw a young woman come out of the morning fog. Water ran from her hair and her clothes. She came onto the porch and tipped milk from the milk can into a deep blue bowl. Then she turned and walked back toward Cliff's End. The morning fog wrapped around her.

"Wait!" cried Martha. "Come back!" The baby's wail seemed part of the wind. "Wait! I can help!"

Martha jumped off the porch and hurried after the woman. She could barely keep her in sight. At the edge of the cliff, the woman turned and looked at Martha. Their eyes met. Martha had never seen eyes like these before. There was such pleading in them, such entreaty, that Martha was frozen where she stood. The young woman moved so quickly—

"Ah, don't!" cried Martha. "Don't!" But the woman was gone.

Martha ran to the cliff's edge. The young woman could not have found her way down the cliff path in the dark, but there was no broken body on the rocks. Instead of a baby's cry, there was a song, a sweet soft croon, along with the sound of the sea.

Joe found Martha kneeling at the edge of the cliff, gazing into the incoming tide. He led her home, wrapped her in a blanket at the kitchen table, and made her some tea. She sat, her hands around the warm cup, thinking and silent. Joe wanted to go for the doctor but feared leaving her alone. He knew he could not bear to bring his wife's body up from the sea the way he had his son's.

"I'm all right, Joe," Martha said finally. "You go on and see to your work. I wasn't thinking of following her into the sea, really. I'm going to sit on the porch."

That's just what she did. She sat there all day, frowning at Cliff's End, listening to the sea.

Joe stayed close to the house and close to Martha. There were enough chores to do. But each time he checked, and it was often, there she sat, frowning toward Cliff's End.

At sunset, Joe joined Martha on the porch.

"There'll be a flood tide tonight. The sea's already coming in fast." He wished the words unsaid as soon as they were spoken. It had been a flood tide that had taken their son by surprise and changed the currents near Cliff's End Beach.

Martha stirred, and there was a sudden light in her eyes.

"That's it, Joe! That's it! That's why!"

She dropped her teacup, and with the blanket still around her shoulders, ran to the edge of the porch. Joe grabbed her wrist to hold her back. She turned and grabbed his shirtfront, shaking him.

"Don't you see, Joe? Don't you see? We've got to go now, before the tide comes in. With a flood tide tomorrow we'll be too late! Now, Joe! We have to go now!"

He followed her. What else could he do? He thought she was mad. He thought the grief had finally caught her. He thought she was having nightmares in the twilight. He didn't know what he thought. He followed her to the edge of the cliff. There was a narrow stone path down to the inlet. Neither had used it since Joe had carried Johnny's body up the cliff face that long year ago, but now both scrambled down to the small strip of beach, visible only

53

at low tide. Martha got there first, gave a small cry, and fell to her knees in the sand. Joe, coming up behind her, saw what she saw. There was the body of a young woman in a dark green dress at the water's edge. Her long hair was tangled in the rocks, and the waves lifted her body, her long dark hair, and the dark green dress.

"Don't look, Martha," said Joe. "Don't look."

She'd seen Johnny's body when he brought it up from the sea. It had been pale and white, without a mark, but Joe knew this woman had been in the water three or four days at least. She'd been pretty once, but not any-more, and Joe didn't want Martha to have someone else to people her dreams. As he untangled the young woman's hair and lifted her from the water, he heard a low wail. He thought it was Martha. She was the only one there. He stumbled from the water and lay the body on the sand, stripping off his jacket to cover the face. Martha was on her feet, looking around, frantic, wring-ing her hands. The low wail came over and over again. It was enough to break his heart.

"But Martha, what is it?" he asked.

Relief flooded Martha's face.

"You hear it, Joe? You really hear it?"

He nodded. "Yes, but what is it? *Where* is it?"

Martha pointed to a low rock shelf set into the cliff just above the tide line, where Johnny would leave his clothes when he went to swim.

"There, Joe, there!"

Joe climbed up. An incoming wave lifted the drowned woman's hair and wet the hem of Martha's skirt. Joe peered into the shelf. For a moment he was still. Then—

"Here, Martha! Catch!" Into her waiting hands he dropped a deep blue bowl. She could still smell the milk it once held.

"I'm coming down. Look out now."

What a picture they must have made. Martha, a drowned woman at her feet, gazing up at her husband as he climbed one-handed down the rocks. Joe stepped carefully, for it grew darker by the moment. Safe on the sand, he turned to his wife.

"Hold out your arms," he said to Martha, and into them he put the baby, just a few weeks old, and quite, quite alive.

"There, there, now," said Martha. "There, there." She made soothing, reassuring noises, wrapping the baby in the blanket she still had around her shoulders.

"Can you bring the mother, Joe? Poor soul, we musn't leave her. The sea's had enough of her already."

Joe followed Martha up the stony path, carrying the drowned woman as gently as Martha carried the child.

They found out later that the young woman came from an inland village. Her husband was a sailor lost at sea. When she'd received the news, the child had just been born. The strain was too much for the new mother. She began to wander in her mind. One moonless night, carrying nothing but her child and the deep blue bowl, she crept out of her village and down to the sea. No one claimed the body, not even the pastor. There was some question as to whether the girl should lay in hallowed ground, you see.

Martha Seton had no questions. She and Joe buried the young mother next to their son, and the flowers that Martha planted on one grave spread to the other.

No one claimed the child, either. Not that Martha would have given her up. It seemed only fair to her that from the sea that had taken her son, she would save a daughter. And when the little girl grew up, Martha told her about the young mother who had loved her child so much, she had defied death and come back to save her from the sea. Martha always took it as a personal kindness that she did so.

SEVEN
Hide and Seek

The house was old. The woman who lived in the house was old. She was old when the parents of the town were children, and when their parents were children, too. The hedge around the house was an old tangled wall. Inside the wall, the topiary garden was overgrown, and the hedge animals needed trimming. The window in the turret that rose above the garden was an old cloudy eye that looked out over the town.

Everyone knew the old woman belonged to the house. She never went out, except into the garden. The hedge grew taller. The house got older. The neighborhood children who tried to sneak into the garden one Halloween tried only once.

"The hedges are alive," they said, and the grown-ups laughed.

"It's just the wind blowing through the garden," the parents said. "The wind shakes the limbs of the hedge animals, that's all."

The children allowed themselves to be comforted, but they never went back to the garden, and they left the old woman strictly alone.

"We know what happens in that house," they would say, but of course they didn't know at all.

Things would have gone on that way, the hedges growing taller, the house getting older, except one day a girl came to live at the house. The neighborhood knew that the girl, Jane, belonged to the house the same way the old woman belonged to the house.

The old woman had the hedges trimmed, the fountain turned on, and the girl enrolled in school. Things might have been fine, but Jane was not invited into the circle of children at the school. It was little Debbie who kept her out.

"Like 'Little Debbie Snack Cakes, I'm so sweet!'" she used to croon.

But she wasn't sweet at all. She was a little beast, especially to the new girl.

"Witch girl," Debbie hissed. "How many old ladies are buried in the garden?"

The other children were curious, but Debbie was just mean.

"Witch girl, ghoul girl, you can never be one of us!"

Thanks to Debbie's poison, Jane was shunned by the other children and left to play by herself. With that sneaky cleverness some children know so well, the names and the nastiness were kept to secret whispers the grown-ups never heard.

Jane escaped the taunts of little Debbie and her followers by slipping through the iron gate into the garden. The old fountain gurgled through the ivy that draped over a cracked basin. The chipped stone cherub smiled over his tangled beds. The hedges were so tall that the garden was a maze. If you wandered in it far enough, you could barely see the house. The children never followed Jane into the garden; they were too frightened to pass through the gate. The hedges hid Jane, although the shrubbery could not block out the taunts: "Witch girl! Ghoul girl! They should burn you, and the old lady, too!"

Jane sat in the garden next to a stone bench. She was so lonely. She put her head down on her arms. She wasn't crying. If she had been crying she would not have heard the rustling in the hedge.

"Who's there?" she called.

She peered into the foliage. The face that looked out at her was made of dark green leaves, and the eyes were greener still. Jane held her breath.

"Don't be afraid," she said. "I won't hurt you."

From that day on the taunts of the other children fell off Jane like dead leaves from a cold tree. She had a friend. Her friend never came into the house, but they played in the garden all the time, tag and dead man's bluff and hide and seek. Hide and seek was her friend's favorite game. The garden rang with Jane's call: "Come out, come out, wherever you are!"

Knowing that her friend would be waiting for her every day after school gave Jane a kind of armor against the children's teasing. Most of them moved on to other games when they failed to drive Jane to tears, but the determined Debbie would not leave her alone. Debbie would follow Jane home, stopping at the wrought-iron gate to whisper hateful things through the metal leaves and blossoms.

"No one will ever like you. No one will ever be your friend. Why don't you just die?"

The closed gate stopped Debbie from entering the garden for a long time, until one special evening.

That evening was like every other. Jane ran into the garden, and Debbie stood outside, hateful and hating.

"Witch girl! Ghoul girl!"

Debbie rattled the gate, and it swung open without a sound. Jane, a lone figure on the path, turned and called out: "Do you want to play with us?"

She took off running between the hedgerows, calling, "Come out, come out, wherever you are!"

A furious Debbie ran after her. "No one plays with you!

You have no friends!"

"Oh, yes I do, yes I do, and his favorite game is hide and seek! Hide and seek! Who hides and who seeks?"

Jane disappeared down a path, and Debbie followed.

"Just wait till I get you! You just wait!"

Debbie ran and ran and ran, the paths went on and on and on, the garden never seemed to end, and the hedges grew taller while the night grew darker. Debbie had to stop running. She leaned on a tree, breathless. When did it get so dark?

"Jane?"

Over the hedges Jane's voice floated on the nighttime air.

"Hide and seek! Hide and seek! Who hides and who seeks?"

The hedges were high. The paths were empty. Debbie could not hear the noises from the street. All she could hear was the wind blowing through the leaves, blowing through the hedge. All she could hear were the rustling leaves, the rustling hedge. Debbie walked back to where the gate should have been. The topiary animals stretched in the wind. The moon came up and glowed through the beastly hedges, giving the overgrown animals eyes that gleamed in the night. Debbie began to run to where the gate ought to have been, to where the street ought to have been, to run from the rustling to the gate, the gate, the gate and the street, but the rustling got louder and the hedges got taller and the rustling got louder and the hedges got taller and the rustling got louder and the hedges got taller.

"Jane! Jane! Where are you?" Debbie shrilled.

There was the gate, the gate, the gate; a short run to the gate and she would be safe. A figure stepped onto the path between Debbie and the gate.

"Jane?"

No. No, not Jane.

"Hide and seek, hide and seek, who hides and who seeks?"

A leaf green face with eyes that glowed with green fire, a leaf green mouth, and a voice that rustled and rustled and rustled.

"Who hides and who seeks?"

The high hedges muffled any noise.

The authorities never found any trace of Debbie, not even when they thought to search the old woman's garden. All they found were topiary animals, overgrown and twisted, and a fountain with a chipped cherub smiling down on the weeds. People's memories being what they are, little Debbie was strangely sweeter in death than she was in life.

When the old woman died, Jane left the old house. But not for long. She came back one day with a little girl. Everyone knew that as the old lady belonged to the house, and Jane belonged to the house, the little girl belonged to the house, too. Jane had the hedges trimmed, the fountain turned on, and the little girl enrolled in school. Even though none of the neighborhood children would play with her, it wasn't long before passersby could hear the little girl calling, "Hide and seek! Hide and seek! Who hides and who seeks?" above the garden hedges. They would think what a pleasant game the little girl was playing.

"Hide and seek! Hide and seek! Who hides and who seeks?"

Come out, come out, wherever you are.

A Note from the Author

The stories in *Passion and Poison* are original tales or retellings based on traditional folkloric motifs. I composed the tales for storytelling, and as such they are meant to be told or read aloud. My intent was not only to reclaim some folkloric ground for anonymous female characters but to discover the emotional truth of the stories being told. True to the traditional idea of the power of names, I discovered that picking specific names for the women in the tales helped me to understand them.

"The Bargain" and "Rosie Hopewell" are based on the traditional motif of shape-shifters, both human and animal.

"The Bargain" is an original version of a New England folktale, a variant of which can be found in *Haunted New England* by Mary Bolte (Chatham Press, 1972).

"Rosie Hopewell," originally written when I was an undergraduate, was reconstituted for a ghost story event at the Illinois Storytelling Festival. The odd thing was that I did not know who the narrator was until the end of the story—it was almost as if the aunt were telling me the story herself.

"Skulls and Bones, Ghosts and Gold" is an extended two-part story based on an English folktale commonly called "The Dauntless Girl." A version of "The Dauntless Girl" can be found in Kevin Crossley-Holland's *British Folktales* (Orchard, 1987). My version not only has newly acquired names for the characters but has the addition of a new character, Ruby, a sister not present in traditional versions of this tale.

"The Severed Hand" is closer to a traditional variant than any other tale in this collection. Joseph Jacobs collected "Mr. Fox," an early version of this tale, for his compilation, *English Fairy Tales* (A. L. Burt, 1895).

"Rubies" is *very* loosely based on the Child ballad "Lady Isabel and the Elf Knight," six versions of which can be found online at:
http://www.springthyme.co.uk/ballads/balladtexts/4_LadyIsabel.html (last accessed on April 24, 2007).

"Sea Child" is based on the folkloric motif of a mother returning from the grave to save her infant from imminent danger. There are variants of this tale in many cultures (English, Scottish, American, Italian, to name just a few), but I could not find a version that suited my sense of the tale, and so I felt compelled to write my own.

"Hide and Seek" was a response to a need for a spooky supernatural tale that included everyday elements. My story features a mysterious supernatural being that is based on the British and European Green Man. The Green Man is said to be a pagan god depicted with a mask or face of foliage, who embodies the spirit of the natural world.